Sleeping Beauty

Retold by Lesley Sims

Illustrated by Sara Gianassi

Reading consultant: Alison Kelly

There was once a king and
queen, who had everything
they could possibly want...

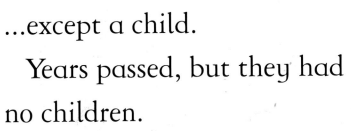

...except a child.

Years passed, but they had
no children.

3

At last, when they had
completely given up hope,
the queen had a beautiful
baby girl.

The proud parents were
delighted. They named her
Rosalind.

"We'll hold a christening," cried the king. "And the grandest feast ever seen!"

Servants sent out
invitations...

...to dukes and
duchesses...

...to lords
and ladies...

...and to the
seven fairies of
the kingdom.

6

"Will you be Rosalind's godmothers?" the king and queen asked the fairies.

They knew that fairies gave the best presents.

After the christening, everyone went into the Great Hall for the feast.

Each fairy was given a
golden plate and goblet,
studded with diamonds
and rubies.

"WAIT!" screeched a voice. A furious fairy swept into the hall. No one had seen her for fifty years.

"Oh dear!" said the king,
who had forgotten about her.

The king leaped up to get
her a plate. The queen rushed
to get her a goblet.

There were no gold ones
left, only plain silver ones.

"How DARE you forget
me!" snarled the fairy.

"Time for the presents!"
said the king, hurriedly.

13

As the crib was moved to
the middle of the room, the
youngest fairy slipped behind
a curtain.

The other fairies lined up
to give their presents.

They showered the baby
princess with wishes.

clever...

You will be graceful...

kind...

beautiful...

a dancer...

a singer...

"My gift now," snarled the old fairy. "At sixteen, you will prick your finger on a spinning wheel and DIE!"

"No!" wailed the queen
and began to weep.

"Oh!" said a duchess and
fainted.

Silence fell. The guests were
too shocked to speak.

The youngest fairy stepped out from behind the curtain.

Please don't cry.

"I cannot stop the spell, but I can soften it.

Princess Rosalind won't die.
She will simply fall asleep.

After one hundred years,
a prince will wake her."

At once, the king declared,
"From this day, all spinning
wheels are banned!"

Bonfires blazed all over the kingdom. Every single spinning wheel burned...

...except one that was hidden.

Princess Rosalind grew up
just as the fairies had wished.

At sixteen years old,
she was clever, graceful
and always kind.

One day, when her parents
were out, Princess Rosalind
decided to explore the palace.

She wandered down long
halls and up dusty stairs...

24

...until she reached a little room at the top of a tower.

There sat an old woman,
spinning wool.

She smiled a sly smile
at Princess Rosalind and
beckoned her closer.

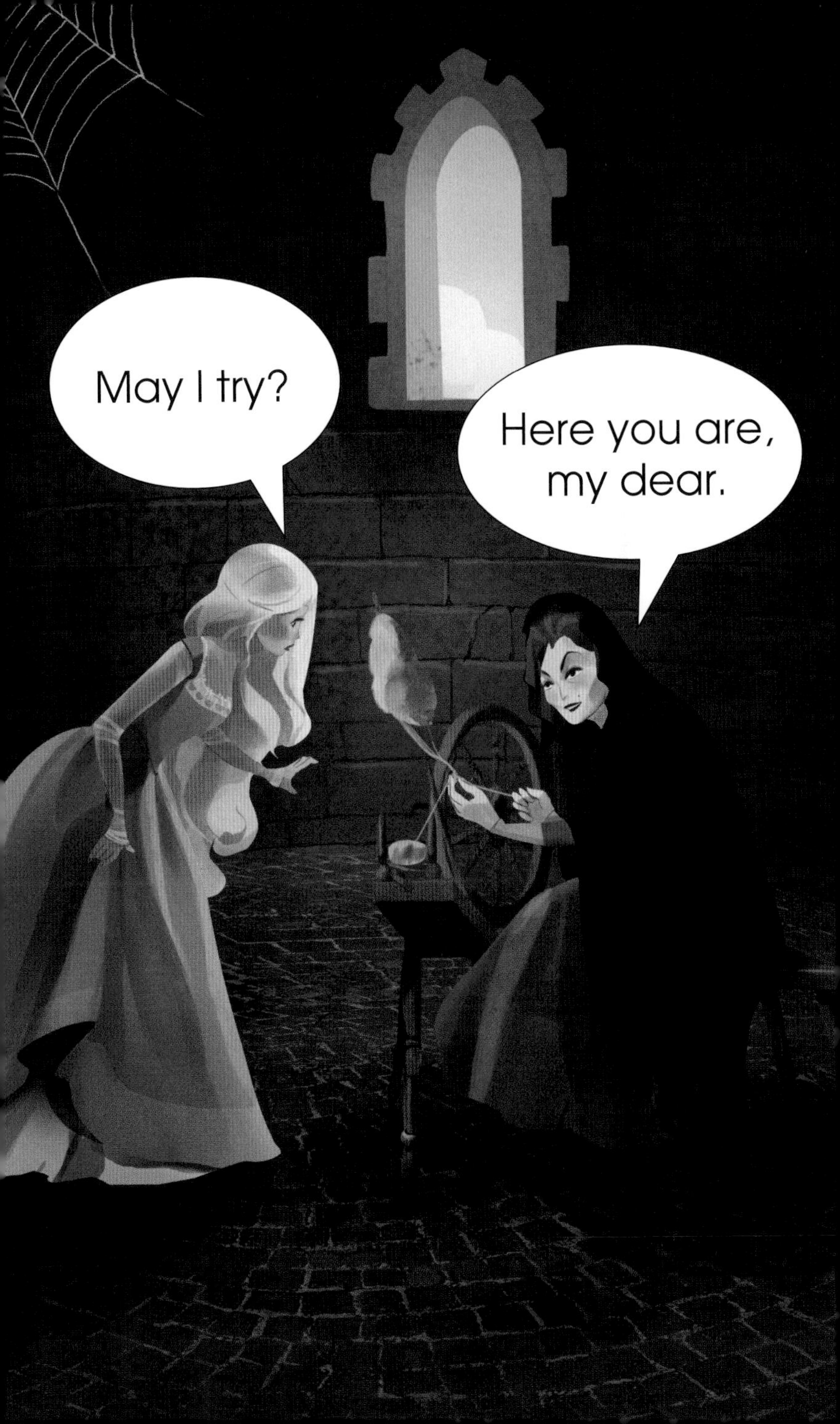
May I try?
Here you are, my dear.

As Rosalind bent over the spinning wheel, she pricked her finger and fell into a deep sleep.

"Ha, ha!" cackled the old woman. She vanished with a BANG!

The noise sent people racing in. They shouted and shook the princess, but no one could wake her.

A maid even threw a jug of cold water over her. Princess Rosalind stayed fast asleep.

Four footmen carried her to bed. The king and queen came home and ran to her.

The youngest fairy heard
the news and flew straight to
the palace.

She knew that the princess
would be lonely when she
woke up.

So she flew around the
palace and sprinkled
everyone with magic.

The cooks in the kitchen
fell asleep.

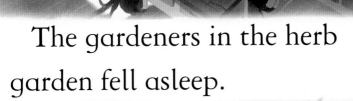

The gardeners in the herb
garden fell asleep.

The stable boys fell asleep
with the horses.

Even the jester
fell asleep in
the middle
of a trick.

Outside, a tangle of trees sprang up around the walls.

Soon a thick forest surrounded the palace. Only the topmost turrets peeked above the trees.

Spiky branches barred
the way. No one could get
through.

One day, a prince was out hunting when he noticed the palace.

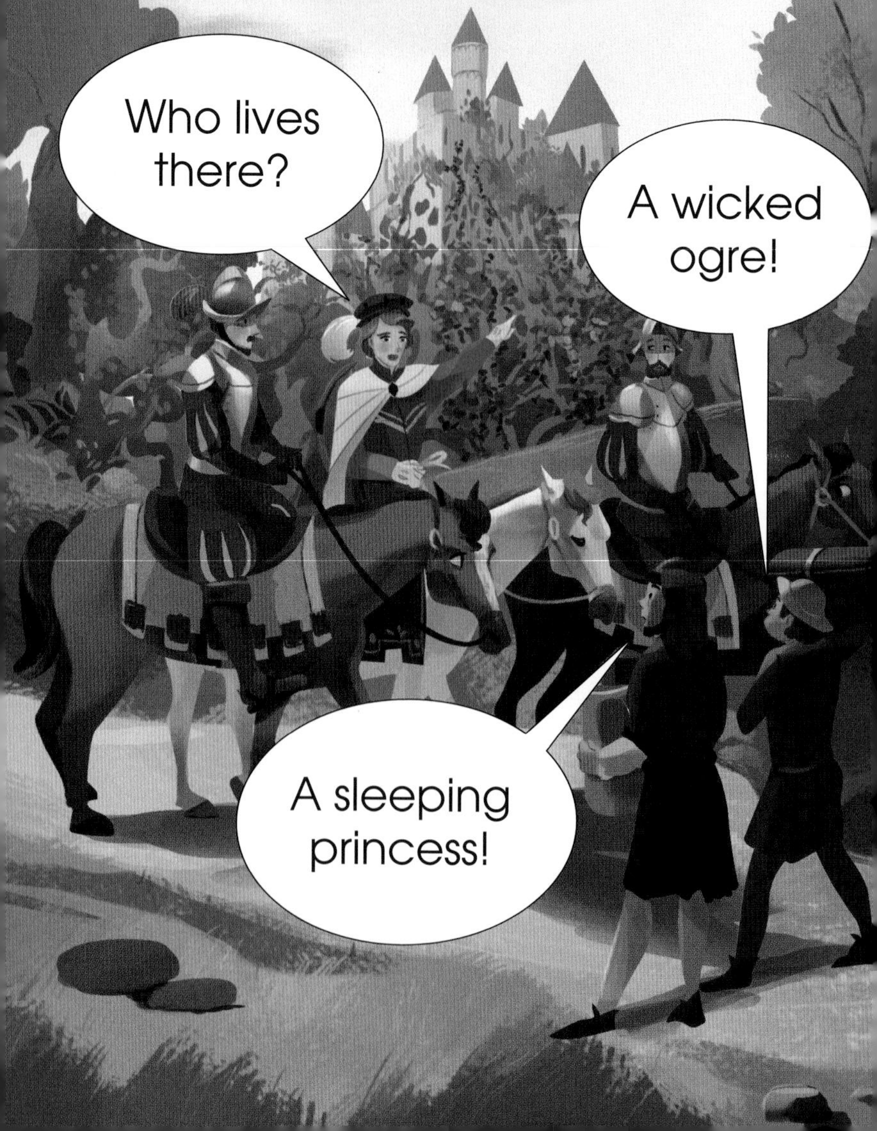

The prince decided to see for himself. He strode up to the forest. Roses burst into bloom and the branches parted.

The prince crept through
the courtyard, past dreaming
doorkeepers and dozing dogs.

He found the Great Hall, with the king and queen and courtiers, all fast asleep.

He wandered through passages and up winding staircases until, at last, he came to the princess's room.

41

"Hello, Princess," he whispered, and Princess Rosalind woke up.

"Who are you?" she asked.

"I'm Prince Leo," he said.

"What happened here?

Everyone is asleep!"

As he spoke, the palace
started to come back to life.

Princess Rosalind found her parents, who told them about the spell.

The queen smiled. "Thank you for rescuing us, Prince Leo. Please stay for a while."

Over time, Princess Rosalind and Prince Leo fell in love. One year later, they married...

...and this time, no grumpy fairies spoiled the party.

About the story

One version of *Sleeping Beauty* was first told
nearly 700 years ago. In that story, the
princess falls asleep when she gets a magic
splinter in her finger. The story in this book
is based upon the tale of a French writer,
Charles Perrault, which was published
in his book of fairy stories in 1697.

Designed by Jodie Smith
Series designer: Russell Punter

First published in 2018 by Usborne Publishing Ltd., Usborne House,
83-85 Saffron Hill, London EC1N 8RT, England. www.usborne.com
Copyright © 2018 Usborne Publishing Ltd.

USBORNE FIRST READING
Level Four

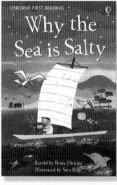

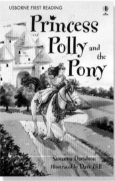